Whiffle Squeek

Whiffle Squeek

Caron Lee Cohen · Illustrated by Ted Rand

DODD, MEAD & COMPANY   New York

Published by Dodd, Mead & Company, Inc.
71 Fifth Avenue, New York, NY 10003
Distributed in Canada by
McClelland and Stewart Limited, Toronto
Printed in the United States of America
1 2 3 4 5 6 7 8 9 10

Library of Congress Cataloging-in-Publication Data

Cohen, Caron Lee.
   Whiffle Squeek.

   Summary: A seafaring cat named Whiffle Squeek has a
narrow escape from a hungry monster of the briny deep.
   [1. Cats—Fiction.   2. Monsters—Fiction.   3. Sea
stories.   4. Stories in rhyme]   I. Rand, Ted, ill.
II. Title.
PZ8.3.C66Wh   1987   [E]   86-32908
ISBN 0-396-08999-2

For Ilene Andler Feldman
—CLC

For Gloria
—TR

There was a cat sailed the briny deep,
Briny deep, briny deep;
There was a cat sailed the briny deep,
And his name was Whiffle Squeek.

He traveled by kibitka boat,
Kibitka boat, kibitka boat;
He traveled by kibitka boat,
And his name was Whiffle Squeek.

He slept beneath the hugeous moon,
Hugeous moon, hugeous moon;
He slept beneath the hugeous moon,
And his name was Whiffle Squeek.

He caught herring with a worm-bait trap,
Worm-bait trap, worm-bait trap;
He caught herring with a worm-bait trap,
And his name was Whiffle Squeek.

His hat was made of octopus arms,
Octopus arms, octopus arms;
His hat was made of octopus arms,
And his name was Whiffle Squeek.

His coat was made of misfit fish,
Misfit fish, misfit fish;
His coat was made of misfit fish,
And his name was Whiffle Squeek.

His pants were made of sea-green weeds,
Sea-green weeds, sea-green weeds;
His pants were made of sea-green weeds,
And his name was Whiffle Squeek.

His boots were made of jellyfish squish,
Jellyfish squish, jellyfish squish;
His boots were made of jellyfish squish,
And his name was Whiffle Squeek.

There was a MONSTER in the briny deep,
Briny deep, briny deep;
There was a MONSTER in the briny deep,
And his name was Gazook Gaboot.

His tail tossed about with a whip-snap flip,
Whip-snap flip, whip-snap flip;
His tail tossed about with a whip-snap flip,
And his name was Gazook Gaboot.

His nose sputtered out with fire and fumes,
Fire and fumes, fire and fumes;
His nose sputtered out with fire and fumes,
And his name was Gazook Gaboot.

His tongue zigzagged with pitchfork prongs,
Pitchfork prongs, pitchfork prongs;
His tongue zigzagged with pitchfork prongs,
And his name was Gazook Gaboot.

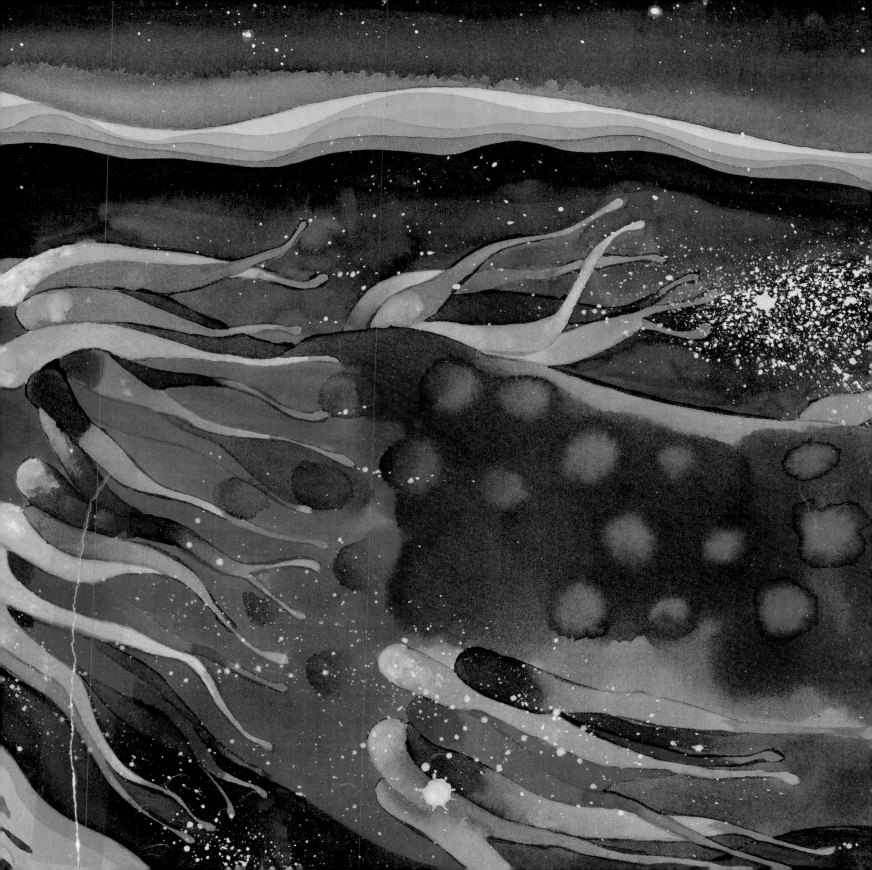

He ate up Whiffle's jellyfish squish,
Jellyfish squish, jellyfish squish;
He ate up Whiffle's jellyfish squish,
And his name was Gazook Gaboot.

He ate up Whiffle's sea-green weeds,
Sea-green weeds, sea-green weeds;
He ate up Whiffle's sea-green weeds,
And his name was Gazook Gaboot.

He ate up Whiffle's misfit fish,
Misfit fish, misfit fish;
He ate up Whiffle's misfit fish,
And his name was Gazook Gaboot.

He ate up Whiffle's octopus arms,
Octopus arms, octopus arms;
He ate up Whiffle's octopus arms,
And his name was Gazook Gaboot.

He ate up Whiffle's worm-bait trap,
Worm-bait trap, worm-bait trap;
He ate up Whiffle's worm-bait trap,
And his name was Gazook Gaboot.

His tummy hurt 'neath the hugeous moon,
Hugeous moon, hugeous moon;
His tummy hurt 'neath the hugeous moon,
And his name was Gazook Gaboot.

He choked on the kibitka boat,
Kibitka boat, kibitka boat;
He choked on the kibitka boat,
And that ENDED Gazook Gaboot!

There was a cat swam home to sleep,
Home to sleep, home to sleep;
There was a cat swam home to sleep,
And his name was Whiffle Squeek.

About the Story

Whiffle Squeek is a story in rhyme. The theme of the story and the rhythm are based on an early nineteenth-century Scottish song. In it a man, Aiken Drum, lived on the moon, and meets a man named Willy Wood, with much the same results as Whiffle Squeek and Gazook Gaboot.

There is very little known about the origins of the song, except that it was common in Scotland in 1821.